# Clouds
## on the
# Mountain

# Clouds
## on the
# Mountain

Story
## Emilie Smith-Ayala

Art
## Alice Priestley

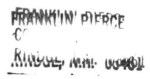

Annick Press Ltd. · Toronto · New York

Annick Press gratefully acknowledges the support of the
Canada Council and the Ontario Arts Council.

The illustrator wishes to thank Mynor Ayala for generously lending his
video footage and photographs of the author's home in Mexico.

**Canadian Cataloguing in Publication Data**

    Smith-Ayala, Emilie
        Clouds on the mountain

    ISBN 1-55037-473-7 (bound) 1-55037-472-9 (pbk.)

    1. Picture books for children.  I. Priestley, Alice.
    II. Title.

    PS8587.M57C56 1996   jC813'.54   C95-932629-4
    PZ7.S66C1 1996

The art in this book was rendered in pencil crayon.
The text was typeset in Times Roman.

Distributed in Canada by:
Firefly Books Ltd.
250 Sparks Avenue
Willowdale, ON
M2H 2S4

Published in the U.S.A. by Annick Press (U.S.) Ltd.
Distributed in the U.S.A. by:
Firefly Books (U.S.) Inc.
P.O. Box 1338
Ellicott Station
Buffalo, NY 14205

*Chac, the Mayan god of rain and thunder,*
*gazed down from his seat among the clouds...*

*For the greatest auntie ever,*
*great, great Auntie Marie, who still hikes in the hills.*
*E.S.A.*

*For my daughter, Ilissa.*
*A.P.*

Abel thundered downstairs and outside, into the breaking day. The sun was slung low, bright and yellow across the valley. Fresh night rains had come and washed the dust down. Through the town and up the mountain, layer on layer of rippled green unrolled, light green, dark green, all of it new.

"Yes!" shouted Abel straight to the big mountain, and he jumped up high, closer to the cloudless sky. Then he tore back into the house— would no one ever get up? Today was the Big Day, when school was finally over, today was the day they were going up the mountain to the waterfall, but everybody was asleep.

Two days ago Bram fell off the monkey bars, and a half-cast had been put on his sore arm.

Then yesterday a friend of Mama's came and left a black ball of fur on the doorstep. Freddie, they called the teeny puppy. She cried all night long until the boys put her under the covers in their own warm bed.

Now at last the Big Day was here, and the sun shone. And at last everyone did get up. Mama made tuna and avocado sandwiches and Abel filled the water bottles—even though there's water at the top, he said. Axelito washed fresh mangoes and grapes. Bram just watched, his arm in a sling.

Freddie cried when they put her in her box lined with an old towel. They were just shutting the front door when she jumped out and ran to them, whining.

"Oh, Mama," said Abel, "we can't just leave her."

So they moved things around in the packs. Mama and Bram took more, and so did Axelito. Then Freddie went into Abel's partly unzipped pack. She wiggled a bit, and yipped so no one would forget she was there. Then she went to sleep.

One, two, three, four blocks they walked, to the soccer field. Next they came to a farmer's field and tiptoed carefully around the new corn plants just peeking out. A pair of orange orioles swept by, happy the dry season was over.

Little butterflies and gigantic ones, orange, yellow and white, fluttered through the air. Down in the town dogs were barking. Over the top of the mountain one little white cloud puffed into view, rimmed with morning gold.

Mama and the boys strolled and hummed. They stopped to pick up little red seeds, acorn caps, pretty stones. They walked along a road, rough and rocky, spotted with knee-deep holes. At the foot of the mountain a few horses stood grazing. The road trickled away into a path that wandered up for a while and then disappeared. Over the top of the mountain two medium-sized grey clouds tumbled into view, heavy and sagging.

Mama wrinkled her forehead. "I can't quite remember the way," she said.

"Don't worry," said Abel. "I know the way."

They crossed a dry river bed, crawling over huge
stones and fallen logs. At last they plunged into the
forest and up the side of the mountain, scrambling now.
Abel went first. He knew the way and he didn't need
help. Axelito kept up, stretching his little legs as far as
they could go. Bram managed with one arm to get up
most rocks by himself.

Suddenly they could hear the echo of falling water.

"We're close!" shouted Abel.

Over the top of the mountain three black clouds
glowered. They were pushing each other over and
rolling higher in the sky.

"I think we should go back," said Mama.

"No!" pleaded the boys.

Bram said he was okay.

"It'll just blow away," promised Abel.

They listened again for the water and followed it higher. Now they were really climbing. Mama and Abel pushed and pulled the littler ones up. Freddie was still asleep in Abel's pack. The black clouds rumbled as if a giant in the sky were clearing its throat. Then—they saw water!

A thin silver stream came tumbling down the rocks to greet them. At last!

They all sat and took off their packs. They drank fresh water, so cold. Freddie woke up and crawled out of her cosy pack. She whimpered once at the boys' feet and then toddled off sniffing.

The sky rumbled again and a gigantic, thick, purple cloud with flashes of fire came coiling and boiling up the other side of the mountain. All at once it devoured the three black clouds, the two grey clouds and the one little white cloud. And then it ate what was left of the wide blue sky.

The rain roared down all at once.

"Hurry up! Hurry up!" shouted Mama. "We've got to go back down."

But it was too late. In a minute they were soaked—right through to their underwear and socks. Axelito started to cry, and Bram did, too. Even Abel knew they were in trouble now.

A bolt of lightning split the sky in two—and right away thunder smashed into the mountains around. The sky was tearing itself to pieces and the earth below was shaking. Mama scooped up Axelito and Abel grabbed Bram by his good arm. They took the first step down.

"But Freddie! Mom, where's Freddie?" cried the boys all at once. Nothing small and black could be seen anywhere. The clouds and the pounding rain had erased the world.

"Freddie! Freddie!" they called. But she was still too little and hadn't learned her own name yet.

Mama put Axelito down for a minute, and huddled the three boys together.

"Where would you go if you were so small?" she asked.

The boys peered through the wall of water. They stared closely at the ground. Then at last they saw the shadow of a small tree, just starting to grow up.

"There she is!" shouted Axelito, pointing underneath. Abel charged the rocks and rescued the shivering puppy, who was doing her best to cry out loud.

"Let's go!" howled Mama, and the lightning crashed again.

Down they went, over the slippery rocks and around the muddy curves.

They came across a cave and crawled
inside. But it was cramped and dark, and big
dangling spider webs hung from the low ceiling.
Further down they found an overhanging ledge
where they stopped and caught their breath. But
now they were so cold and wet that everyone just
wanted to go home. The rain poured down still,
like ice from the sky. But they were on their way.

The river bed lay before them, with swirling water in it this time. Abel threw a small stick in and the current roared and ripped it downstream.

"It's too deep," said Axelito.

"Not if I hold you up high," said Mama.

Across they went, two and two, Mama carrying them through the fast water. Then the road appeared, and they heard the wet neigh of the horses.

As they walked into the cornfield the rain dripped and finally stopped.

"Chac must have seen us and been sorry," said Abel.

Everyone turned and looked at the mountain. They couldn't see the top: it still swirled with clouds. They limped across the soccer field. Now their heavy shoes squish–squish–squished even more than the soaking grass. From the soccer field they counted blocks: four, three, two, one.

They all had a shower. Then they went into
Mama's big bed with hot, hot chocolate and watched
cartoons all afternoon.

Everyone was glad to be dry again, especially
Freddie!